DRAGONS
AND OTHER
LEGENDARY
MONSTERS

AN INTREPID WANDERER'S GUIDE

...ncyclopedia Company

Bright Connections Media
A World Book Encyclopedia Company
233 North Michigan Avenue
Chicago, Illinois 60601
U.S.A.

For information about other BCM publications, please
visit our website at http://www.brightconnectionsmedia.com
or call 1-800-967-5325.

Dragons and Other Legendary Monsters:
An Intrepid Wanderer's Guide
ISBN: 978-1-62267-025-3

Printed in China by Toppan Leefung Printing Ltd.,
Guangdong Province
1st printing August 2013

Picture credits:
All illustrations © Amber Books Ltd (Illustrator Myke Taylor/The Art
Agency) except pages 6-7, 20-21, 30-33, 38-41, 52-61, 70-83, 86-91 © IMP AB

Contents

INTRODUCTION

For as long as humans have had fears, there have been stories about monsters. Some monsters were born of literature and myth—creatures such as the cyclops, the Sphinx, and the Minotaur. For ancient people, these were not mere fantasies, but real beliefs that haunted their lives. Members of many American Indian tribes, for example, would tremble in fear of the Thunderbird every time a storm slashed through the sky.

Legends of many ancient monsters survived to terrorize people born hundreds of years later. The basilisk, a lethal hybrid creature first described 2,000 years ago by the Roman writer Pliny the Elder, was still feared and encountered by the 1500's. In 1587, a basilisk was said to have killed two young girls who were hiding in a cellar in Poland.

But haven't we moved on since then? Don't we know now that monsters are just products of fantasy?

Don't be so sure. Several of the monsters in this book are certainly figures of pure invention. But countless witnesses throughout history have claimed that monsters are every bit as real as you or me—they have seen them with their own eyes! Thousands of people, for example, say they have seen the Loch Ness Monster. Scientists still aren't able to explain the sightings and huge footprints of Bigfoot. And more than 1,000 people claimed to witness the Jersey Devil in 1909.

All monster stories lurk somewhere between fantasy and reality. Everyone knows that some creatures are pure myth, but people love to hear a good story. Oftentimes, skeptics discredit modern monster stories by giving scientific explanations—Bigfoot, they might argue, is just a big ape. But what's so wrong with believing? Thousands of witnesses can't all be lying, right? Don't let the skeptics fool you. It's human nature to be interested in the unknown, and many people—even the nonbelievers—secretly want to believe in these strange beasts.

BASILISK

The basilisk is a horrific mix of reptile and bird. It is hatched from an egg laid by a rooster, which is then incubated by a toad.

WINGS
In some descriptions, the wings are more like those of a dragon than of a bird.

COMB
The bright, pointed rooster's comb on the head resembles a king or queen's crown.

BODY
This is rounded like a rooster's but has few feathers. Its skin is as scaly as that of the roughest snake.

EYES
Some say the eyes glow a fiery red, like hot coals. Whatever their color, they are deadly.

BEAK
In many accounts, the beak is lined with dagger-like teeth.

TONGUE
Some people say the basilisk has a forked tongue, like a snake.

CLAWS
The beast runs swiftly on feet that bristle with horrendously sharp claws.

With their snakelike bodies, rooster heads, and stumpy wings, basilisks have terrifying magical powers. Just the stare of a basilisk is said to be able to kill people, as is its foul, poisonous breath. It pollutes waterways and turns fertile farmland into barren desert. Rocks shatter if the basilisk brushes against them.

There are few ways to kill a basilisk. Weasels are said to be immune to basilisk magic and poison. If a basilisk is confronted with a mirror, it will be killed by its own reflection.

ACTUAL SIZE

TAIL
The tail is long and snaky, and may even be lined with barbed spines.

DID YOU KNOW?

- In Warsaw, Poland, in 1587, a basilisk was blamed for killing two small girls in a cellar. Reportedly, a prisoner killed the creature with a mirror.

- The idea that a weasel can kill a basilisk may come from tales of the mongoose, a small mammal that preys on snakes.

WHERE IN THE WORLD?

The Roman writer Pliny the Elder described the basilisk nearly 2,000 years ago, but the creature may be even older. People throughout Europe walked in terror of meeting it right up until the 1500's, when the famous naturalist Konrad Gesner denounced it as "gossip."

BEOWULF'S DRAGON

The epic poem *Beowulf* tells of a terrifying dragon that lies coiled in a cavern beneath a gray rock. The dragon, a firedrake measuring 50 feet long, guards a lair filled with priceless treasures.

TAIL
The barbed tail, shaped like an arrowhead, can be used as a weapon in battle. In flight, the tail operates like a rudder, balancing the dragon and allowing it to execute skillful aerial maneuvers.

EYES
Adapted to see in the dim light of caves, the dragon's eyes are well suited for watching over its hoard of plundered treasure.

JAWS
Its fiery breath lights the skies. Armor provides no defense against its crushing jaws and poisonous fangs. A reservoir of venom is located in the upper jaw.

WINGS

Batlike wings attached to the torso by robust muscles lift the dragon in flight. The bones within the wing structure are hollow to reduce their weight. However, they are tougher than reinforced concrete.

BODY

The dragon's enormous body is blackened by the soot of its own flames. Its blue-green scales glow with inner fire.

The poem describes how, after a thief steals a golden cup from its lair, the dragon rampages through the countryside. The firedrake breathes flames that light up the sky, terrifying villagers and burning every home in Geatland. Beowulf, King of the Geats, armed with a magic sword, leads an army into battle to face the dragon.

Beowulf strikes the dragon with his sword, but the blow glances off the beast's terrible hide. Beowulf is engulfed in dragon flames, a sight so terrifying that his army flees. Only the faithful Wiglaf remains to help. Beowulf breaks off the blade of his magic sword in the dragon's head. Beowulf is bitten on the neck by the dragon, but continues fighting. Wiglaf stabs the dragon in a vulnerable place and Beowulf slashes it through the middle, cutting the monster in two and ending its life.

At the end of the poem, Beowulf dies from his battle wounds. The dragon's treasure is buried with him.

Did you know?

- *Beowulf* was probably written in the A.D. 700's. It is considered the first great work of English literature.

- Wooden shields, such as the one Wiglaf used, are a poor choice when doing battle with a firedrake. The dragon's flames are so intense that they burned Wiglaf's shield down to its handle.

- Smoke rising from the mouth of a cave is usually a telltale sign that a dragon resides within.

- The dragon is the largest-known flying creature.

- Hundreds of years ago, dinosaur fossils were believed to be dragon bones.

ACTUAL SIZE

Where in the world?

Geatland, a region in the south of Sweden, is where Beowulf met the mighty dragon in battle. Geatland's deep forests provided the ideal habitat for a firedrake.

● SWEDEN

GORYNYCH

This savage Russian dragon has three fire-spitting heads and seven tails. Gorynych walks on his two hind legs and has two small front legs, like a *Tyrannosaurus rex*. His iron claws can slash through any shield or suit of armor. The air around Gorynych reeks of sulfur, a sign of his evil.

HEADS
Three fanged, fire-spitting heads with terrible horns make it impossible to approach Gorynych. Six watchful eyes and a heightened sense of smell enable him to detect a maiden from a mile away.

CLAWS
Iron claws rip knights' suits of armor open as if they were aluminum cans.

WINGS
Although his great bulk prevents him from flying quickly, Gorynych's wings allow him to descend in places where he is least expected.

TAILS
Seven wildly thrashing tails render the dragon's back end as hazardous as his front.

BODY
The scaly body produces a reek of sulfur that hangs around Gorynych like a sinister cloud.

Gorynych   13

Russian folk tales tell Gorynych's story. His uncle, the sorcerer Nemal Chelovek, kidnapped the czar's daughter and intended her to wed Gorynych.
The princess was imprisoned in the sorcerer's dark mountain castle. Nemal Chelovek left his fortress unguarded because he believed no one would dare approach him.

The czar offered a reward to anyone who could rescue the princess from the castle. Many princes tried and failed. Ivan, a palace guard who understood the speech of animals, overheard two crows discussing where the princess was hidden. The czar gave Ivan a magic sword to help him on his rescue mission.

The sorcerer turned himself into a giant when he discovered Ivan in his castle. The magic sword flew from Ivan's hands, killing the giant, then flew through the castle halls until it found and slew Gorynych. Ivan then married the princess.

DID YOU KNOW?

- Gorynych caused eclipses of the sun and moon. The fact that they reappeared showed that even a powerful dragon could not defeat the sun and moon. The Russians took this as a sign that dragons can be defeated by the righteous.

- Not all Slavic dragons are destructive. The Slovenian city of Ljubljana is protected by a dragon. This benevolent dragon is pictured on the city's coat of arms.

- Dragon blood is so venomous that Earth does not absorb it.

- There are no cave paintings of dragons because caves are a favorite residence of dragons. A dragon residing in the cave would have driven all cave painters away.

- A magic sword that enables the warrior to stand far away from the dragon is the ideal weapon for battling dragons.

ACTUAL SIZE

WHERE IN THE WORLD?

The fearsome seven-tailed Gorynych is featured in folktales and myths originating from Russia and Ukraine.

● RUSSIA

● UKRAINE

KRAK'S DRAGON

Polish legends tell of a fearsome dragon that lived in a dark cave at the foot of Wawel Hill along the banks of the Vistula River. Every day it raged through the countryside, terrifying the inhabitants of Krakow.

TAIL

The swishing tail knocks over fences, damages bridge supports, and strips bark from trees. It can also crush a human's ribcage with a single blow.

WINGS

Broad wings enable airborne attacks, which are the most effective method of terrorizing the countryside.

HEAD
The dragon's massive skull is counterbalanced in flight by its long tail. Its piercing vision allows it to spot its next meal from half a mile away.

JAWS
Terrible, fire-belching jaws are lined with pointed fangs. The dragon's scorch marks deface barns, forests, public buildings, and flocks of sheep throughout Krakow.

CLAWS
Hooked claws shred and dig into the flesh of the dragon's helpless prey as it holds its squirming meal in its toothy jaws.

KRAK'S DRAGON   17

In legends, this bad-tempered, fire-breathing dragon eats animals and people. Anything that runs from it is fair game. After it gobbles down several small children, it plunders homes for prized possessions to take back to its cave. Many bold knights try to slay this dragon and perish in flames for their efforts. Its daily thefts begin to affect the local economy.

The stories tell of Krak, a cunning peasant boy who has unique culinary skills. The king is desperate for anyone's dragon-slaying services and allows the boy to try. Krak stuffs three roasted sheep full of sulfur and hot spices and leaves the meal near the dragon's cave. The greedy dragon gulps down the meal, which burns its stomach. It drinks half the Vistula River to quench its thirst. The dragon's swollen, burning gut bursts and kills it. Krak marries the princess and is given the dragon's treasure.

Did you know?

- The city of Krakow is named after the heroic Krak.

- Near the cavern beneath the castle of Krakow, there is a monument to Krak's dragon. The statue of the dragon has been fitted with a natural gas nozzle so that it breathes fire every few minutes.

- Many dragons prefer to sleep on top of a pile of jewels and treasure because more traditional bedding materials are too easily ignited by their fiery breath.

- Trickery is often the preferred method for defeating the most dangerous dragons. Cunning is generally a mightier weapon than a sword when facing a beast of such tremendous size, aggression, and appetite.

ACTUAL SIZE

Where in the World?

Every citizen of Poland is familiar with the stories of the death, trauma, and destruction caused by Krak's dragon.

POLAND

ONI

Whistling gaily as it works, this ghastly creature delights in tormenting the people of Japan. It avoids detection by flitting invisibly through the air or taking human form.

HORNS
Onis usually have three horns: either like those of a bull or taking the form of writhing snakes with venomous fangs.

FACE
Some Onis have the heads of cattle or horses, but most have humanlike features—with three eyes and a hideous hole of a mouth that stretches from ear to ear.

HANDS
Onis are immensely strong and can tear down walls with their sharp claws.

FANGS
Onis have long, curved fangs like those of a tiger, and in some tales they are said to gorge on human flesh.

Once a Shinto god, the Oni became an evil spirit after Buddhism spread into Japan from China in the A.D. 500's. In earthly guise, it is said to cause disasters, famine, and disease. In its demonic form, it steals sinners' souls. Female Onis take the form of beautiful women, and they are prone to violent outbursts of rage.

Many Onis have green or red skin. They suffer continual hunger and often have enormous bellies. They are said to hunt down sinners and take them to hell in a fiery chariot.

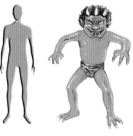

ACTUAL SIZE

DID YOU KNOW?

- A woman may turn into an Oni under the stress of jealousy or grief, while other Onis may be the souls of people who died of plague or famine.

- The Buddhist sage Nichiren regarded the Onis as a punishment for the sins of the Japanese, so he founded a school to reform people.

WHERE IN THE WORLD?

Onis living in the mortal world are found almost exclusively in Japan, although they are thought to have originated in China. Other Onis known as Gaki inhabit the spirit world or Jigoku (hell) underground.

JAPAN

OROCHI

Japanese legends tell of the evil dragon Orochi, who demands that a maiden be offered to him in sacrifice each year. Even the bravest of warriors cannot defeat this vicious, cunning beast.

TAILS
Eight curving tails create strange whistling noises as Orochi thrashes them in anger.

BELLY
Perpetually bloody and inflamed from his kills, the ravenous dragon's belly must always be filled.

BODY
The giant body stretches over eight valleys and eight hills. Orochi's back is covered with moss and trees.

EYES
Eight sets of eyes that are as red as winter cherries keep watch in all directions.

Orochi is described in Japanese legends. His gigantic body slithers across eight hills and valleys, and his eight hungry heads make him impossible to approach. One day Susanoo, the god of the sea and storms, comes upon two weeping parents. Seven of their daughters have been devoured by Orochi in the past seven years. Now their eighth and only remaining daughter is to be sacrificed to Orochi. Susanoo agrees to slay the dragon if their eighth daughter will be his wife.

In the story, Susanoo transforms the maiden into a comb, which he safely hides in his hair. Susanoo arranges eight enormous vats of rice wine in a circle and leaves them out to tempt the dragon. Attracted by the smell of the strong wine, Orochi plunges each of his eight heads into a vat and drinks greedily. The drunken dragon collapses helpless to the ground and Susanoo uses his powerful sword to slice Orochi to pieces. The local river runs red with the blood of the slain menace.

Did you know?

- The dragon's full name, Yamata no Orochi, means "big snake of eight branches."

- Young maidens are a favorite meal of dragons worldwide.

- During the Edo period (1603–1868), it was popular for Japanese firefighters to get dragon tattoos. They believed the image of the dragon would protect them while fighting fires.

- Although fearsome and powerful, Japanese dragons are also fair and benevolent. The Japanese believe dragons bring wealth and good luck.

- Images of dragons adorn many Buddhist temples in Japan. Dragons are thought to dispel evil.

- Glass was once thought to be solidified dragon breath.

ACTUAL SIZE

Where in the World?

Orochi's eight hungry heads terrorized the citizens of Izumo Province in Japan near the foot of Mount Sentsuzan.

JAPAN

St. George's Dragon

This bloodthirsty dragon was said to live by a spring that provided all the water for the northern African city of Cyrene.

HEAD
The solid, thick skull contains eyes with extra optic nerves for keen vision and nostrils that belch foul black fumes.

NECK
An elongated neck keeps the dragon's fire-breathing apparatus at a safe distance from its own body. It also aids in spotting tender maidens and scrappy saints from around corners.

TAIL
A flick of this dragon's razor-sharp tail leaves a man with bloodied stumps where he once had limbs.

WINGS
Wing bones attached to the broad back by a system of mighty muscles lift the heavy beast into the air.

CLAWS
Sturdy talons leave telltale gouges in the turf wherever the dragon walks.

BODY
Scales like steel plates on the dragon's body shatter St. George's spear when he first attempts to stab the creature.

According to legend, the dragon grew unhappy with the diet of sheep the citizens fed it. It demanded daily human sacrifices. Otherwise, it would not allow anyone to draw water from the spring. People drew lots to determine the daily victim. When the princess was chosen as the next victim, her father, the king, became distraught. He offered the citizens all his riches if they would spare his daughter, but the citizens refused.

The princess was tied to a wooden stake near the spring. St. George, a soldier of the Roman Empire, discovered the princess and untied her. St. George attacked the dragon, but his lance only wounded the foul creature. Using the princess's sash as a leash, St. George and the princess led the injured dragon into town. St. George announced he would finish off the dragon if the citizens converted to Christianity. After they agreed to convert, St. George drew his sword and killed the dragon.

Did you know?

- St. George is the patron saint of England, knights, archers, and butchers.

- The flag of Wales bears the image of a red dragon. It has been a Welsh symbol for thousands of years.

- Dragoon soldiers carried a musket, called the dragon. The musket was given this name because it emitted flames when fired.

- The various parts of the dragon are believed to have magical properties. Anyone who eats a dragon's heart gains the ability to understand the speech of birds. Eating dragon's tongue gives one the power to win any argument. Drinking dragon's blood provides protection against injury from swords.

ACTUAL SIZE

Where in the World?

This dragon was believed to nest at a spring that provided water for the citizens of Cyrene, Libya, which is situated in northern Africa.

LIBYA

WEREWOLF

An innocent-looking human by day, a werewolf changes into a terrifying wolfish beast by night. It attacks victims with vicious claws and fangs, tearing the flesh from their bones, or digs up corpses from cemeteries to satisfy its ravenous hunger for human flesh. Belief in werewolves was particularly strong in medieval Europe.

HAIR
Coarse hair coats the body. Some hair may remain even when the monster has reverted to human form.

BODY
When the transformation is complete, the human body has turned into that of a wolflike beast.

EYES
Menacing eyes shine wildly in the moonlight.

TEETH
Large canine fangs and sharp teeth easily sever flesh from bone.

During the day, werewolves are said to look like regular people. However, the light of the full moon will activate the curse. The victim is racked with sudden pain and a terrifying change takes place. His jaws stretch, his teeth enlarge into fangs, and hair breaks through his skin. He scrabbles wildly at his clothing with sharp, glinting claws. When dawn breaks, the werewolf will turn back into a man, blissfully unaware of his earlier crimes.

The belief in werewolves probably grew from the fear of wolves, whose ghostly howls could be heard through the nighttime forests. Belief in werewolves was particularly strong in medieval Europe, and hundreds of innocent people were executed by fearful mobs. Some people really believed they were werewolves and confessed to their "crimes." In fact, they were suffering from a mental illness known as lycanthropy.

Did you know?

- In medieval Europe, people were regularly tried for being werewolves. One of the last convictions took place in 1720 in Salzburg, Austria.

- Many people believed that werewolves disguised themselves by hiding their hair inside their bodies. Suspects were often torn apart as prosecutors searched for evidence.

- Folk stories from around the world tell of people who change into tigers, leopards, hyenas, and bears. Some even describe werepigs, which attack and bite passers-by.

- In European folklore, werewolves sometimes turn into vampires as they die, continuing their reign of terror.

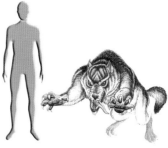

ACTUAL SIZE

Where in the World?

Werewolf legends arose in many parts of Europe, Asia, and North America inhabited by true wolves. The forests of France inspired the most stories: 30,000 cases were reported between 1520 and 1630.

NORTH AMERICA

EUROPE
ASIA

Wyvern

The wyvern is a two-legged British dragon. Wyverns are small and harmless as babies, but don't be fooled! They grow up to be vicious, bloodthirsty adults.

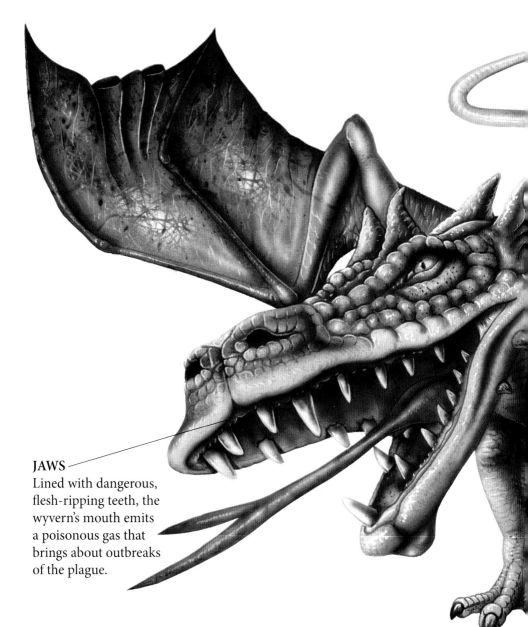

JAWS
Lined with dangerous, flesh-ripping teeth, the wyvern's mouth emits a poisonous gas that brings about outbreaks of the plague.

TAIL

A pointed tail adds to the wyvern's terrifying appearance and inflicts deep wounds on its prey.

WINGS

The wyvern unfolds its broad wings and flaps them furiously while hissing, creating an effect guaranteed to paralyze its victims with fear.

BODY

Although not the largest of dragons, the wyvern is surprisingly well armored. Its shiny scales fend off most lances and projectiles.

CLAWS

Curved talons provide a firm grip on the carcasses that the wyvern flies back to its lair.

A British legend tells of young Maud, who discovered a baby wyvern while walking in the woods near Mordiford. Its body was no bigger than a cucumber and it was covered in sparkling green scales. Maud took the helpless wyvern home, but her parents refused to let her keep it. Maud placed the creature in her secret hiding place in the woods. She visited it daily, feeding it milk and playing with it. The wyvern grew rapidly and soon milk was not enough to satisfy its appetite.

According to the story, the wyvern quickly acquired a taste for human flesh, but remained gentle with Maud. Garston, a man from one of Mordiford's best families, rode out to slay the wyvern. His sturdy shield protected Garston from the flame-spouting wyvern. Garston pierced the beast's shiny scales with his sword, fatally wounding the creature. Maud kneeled on the bloodied grass beside the wyvern. Weeping, she cradled her dying friend in her arms.

DID YOU KNOW?

- Because of their flesh-eating habits, wyverns make terrible pets. Although they are harmless as babies, a dragon's bloodthirsty instincts always set in when it reaches adulthood.

- The wyvern is associated with war, pestilence, and envy. It is believed to bring outbreaks of the plague wherever it goes.

- Its traits of strength, power, and endurance made the wyvern a popular symbol on medieval coats of arms. Its image on shields was used to strike fear into the hearts of enemies.

- British dragons have been known to inhabit places as diverse as caves, fields, woods, swamps, gullies, moors, corn stacks, water holes, and abbey ruins.

- The coat of arms of Moscow bears the image of a soldier on horseback spearing a wyvern.

ACTUAL SIZE

WHERE IN THE WORLD?

In medieval Mordiford, Herefordshire, in England, wyverns were plentiful. It seemed almost anyone could stumble across one with little effort.

ENGLAND

CYCLOPS

The single eye of the cyclops stares menacingly from its horrible, hairy face. This cruel, watchful giant can smash a human to pieces with a single flick of the wrist.

EYE
One huge, watchful eye stares from the center of the cyclops's forehead.

ARMS
Bulging with muscles, its long arms pound out metal and shift stone blocks with ease.

CLAWS
Instead of nails, hooked claws grow from its fingers and toes. If the cyclops is in a bad mood, these make formidable weapons.

HAIR
Sprouting wildly from the cyclops's head, the dirty, matted hair is infested with lice.

TEETH
When the cyclops wants a snack, he rips up humans with his big, pointed teeth.

FEET
The ground shakes when the cyclops stamps his massive feet.

In Greek mythology, the first cyclopes were three brothers called Steropes, Brontes, and Arges. They were the sons of the earth goddess Gaea and the sky god Uranus. They were blacksmiths by trade. The last race of cyclopes were shepherds who lived squalid lives in dingy caves in Sicily, tending their flocks and tearing intruders apart.

The cyclops Polyphemus was said to be the most dreadful of all. In the *Odyssey,* an ancient Greek poem, Polyphemus imprisons the adventurer Odysseus and his men in his cave. The fierce cyclops kills two men each day. Cunning Odysseus devises a plan. He waits for Polyphemus to fall asleep. Then the hero sharpens a stake and heats it in the fire. Driving the weapon into the scary giant's eye, Odysseus twists the stake around, blinding Polyphemus. The survivors escape the next day, clinging to the bellies of the cyclops's sheep as he sends them out to graze.

Did you know?

- The word "cyclops" comes from the Greek words kyklos ("circle") and ops ("eye"). The names of the cyclopes Brontes, Steropes, and Arges mean "thunder," "lightning bolt," and "lightning flash."

- The cyclops myth may have its origins in an ancient guild of Greek metal workers in Thrace, who had circles tattooed on their foreheads.

- Some people believe that the legend of the cyclopes arose when the Ancient Greeks first encountered elephants.

ACTUAL SIZE

Where in the World?

Cyclopes were said to live in the regions of Thrace in northeast Greece, in Lycia in southwest Turkey, and on the island of Crete. They worked in Hephaestus' forge on Lemnos and built the cities of Mycenae and Tiryns. Later tales place them on Mount Etna in Sicily.

MYCENAE & TIRYNS

Thrace

Lemnos

Mount Etna

Lycia

Crete

FAFNIR

Scandinavian mythology tells of Fafnir, a simple dwarf warped by greed. Fafnir and his brother Regin wanted their father's treasure. Fafnir murdered his father and refused to share the treasure with Regin. Years of gloating transformed Fafnir from a dwarf into a terrible dragon.

WINGS
Enormous, leathery wings carry Fafnir's heavy body through the air, enabling him to dive at his victims in surprise attacks from above.

MOUTH
Fafnir's breath is a combination of poisonous gases and flames. His toxic breath is produced in his second stomach.

BELLY
The dragon's only vulnerable spot is his soft stomach. It is sometimes encrusted with jewels from resting on top of his treasure heap for so long.

Regin asked the legendary hero Sigurd to slay Fafnir. Sigurd knew that he needed a strong sword to penetrate the dragon's tough, scaly hide. He repaired his father's broken sword, making it unbreakable and sturdy enough to split an anvil.

According to the story, Sigurd hid in a trench and thrust his mighty sword into Fafnir's belly as the beast slithered overhead. Sigurd cut out Fafnir's heart and roasted it. Fafnir's blood gave Sigurd the power to understand the language of birds. The birds warned Sigurd that Regin planned to kill him, so Sigurd killed Regin and claimed the treasure.

ACTUAL SIZE

DID YOU KNOW?

- Until Sigurd came along, Fafnir was thought to be undefeatable. Numerous brave men went seeking the dragon's treasure but were burned alive and eaten.

- Fafnir's father was the king of the Dwarf Folk. Several Norse gods gave Fafnir's father his treasure as payment for accidentally killing one of Fafnir's brothers.

HIDE
Scales as strong as iron protect Fafnir's body. Many a sword has broken against his armorlike hide.

WHERE IN THE WORLD?

According to Norse mythology, Fafnir crouched atop his heap of hoarded treasure in a cold, dark Norwegian cave.

NORWAY

FUTS-LUNG

In Chinese mythology, Futs-Lung is the dragon of hidden treasures. He lives deep within the earth, guarding precious gems and priceless metals in his lair.

BODY
Futs-Lung can transform himself into any shape he desires or make himself completely invisible. He creates new hills when he hunches his back underground.

EYES
The dragon's bulging eyes can see into the depths of the earth where his treasure is stored.

JAWS
Futs-Lung's voice is like the jingling of copper pans, banging gongs, or ringing bells, depending upon his mood. His furious roar brings forth earthquakes.

FIN

The scalloped dorsal fin along the length of his back stabilizes the dragon as he maneuvers through the air, water, and earth at lightning-fast speeds.

CHIN

Hidden beneath his chin is the pearl of wisdom. The pearl glows from within and is a vessel of health.

Like most Chinese dragons, Futs-Lung is said to be benevolent until he is offended. His wrath should not be roused. He must be treated with respect and reverence so he does not unleash his incredible temper. Volcanoes are formed when Futs-Lung bursts from the earth and reports to heaven. Futs-Lung possesses a magic pearl that represents wisdom. It is considered the most valuable of all his treasures.

Stories say that it takes 3,000 years for Futs-Lung to grow to his terrific adult size. Newly hatched, he looks much like an eel. By 500 years of age, Futs-Lung has grown a head that resembles a carp's. By his 1,500th birthday, he will grow a long tail, a head with a thick beard, and four stumpy legs with claws. At the age of 2,000, Futs-Lung will have horns.

DID YOU KNOW?

- Imperial Chinese dragons have five toes, Korean dragons have four, and Japanese dragons have three.

- Chinese dragons lay one egg at a time. Each dragon egg takes 1,000 years to hatch.

- The Chinese refer to themselves as "descendants of the dragon."

- Chinese dragons have 117 scales on their serpentine bodies.

- Chinese dragons are shape-shifters that can change into the form of a human, shrink themselves down to a mouse, or expand until they fill up the space between the sky and Earth.

- A Hong Kong apartment complex was built near a mountain where Futs-Lung lives. The complex has a large gap in the middle so that Futs-Lung's ocean view would remain unobstructed and his goodwill would be maintained.

ACTUAL SIZE

WHERE IN THE WORLD?

Futs-Lung is the underworld dragon of China. He is in charge of guarding all the precious metals and gems buried in earth.

● CHINA

GRIFFIN

This ferocious mythological beast has the head, wings, and forelegs of an eagle and the hindquarters of a lion. Given to attacking other animals at will, it is also said to tear up humans on sight with its slashing claws and tearing beak.

WINGS
Although the male griffin is often described as wingless, the female has wings like a great eagle. In some tales she flies like a bird, but in others she only takes to the air with short hops when fighting.

HIND PARTS
The griffin has the back end of a lion, and its hair varies in color from gold to cream with scarlet flecks.

TAIL
The long, snakelike tail is tipped with a tuft of hair like that of a lion.

HEAD
The griffin usually has an eagle's head, with terrible piercing eyes and a sharp, curving beak.

EARS
Early Mesopotamian images show the griffin with a crested head, but in later pictures it has feathered, pointed ears.

TALONS
Huge, pointed talons as long as antelope's horns grow from the toes of the forefeet. These are often said to possess magical powers.

The griffin is described as a colossally powerful predator that can carry off a yoke of oxen in its claws. In some medieval accounts, it is stronger than 8 lions and 100 eagles. It also hoards gold and emeralds, fiercely attacking anyone who tries to steal from its nest.

Many griffins were said to live in the ancient land of Scythia, north of the Black Sea—an area rich in gold and jewels. Digging up these treasures with their claws, griffins used them to line their nests. The Arimaspians wanted these riches, too, and often rode on horseback into battle with the griffins. As a result, griffins attacked horses whenever they could. Gripping with their scythe-like claws, they dug in with their hooked bills, leaving terrible, bloody wounds.

Did you know?

- Artifacts from Ancient Greece sometimes show the griffin with a mane of tightly coiled curls.

- One Norse legend tells of Prince Hagen, who was carried away to a griffin's nest. Fortunately, he found a suit of armor and managed to kill the young griffins as they attacked.

- The female griffin lays eggs like those of an eagle.

ACTUAL SIZE

Where in the World?

Griffins were thought to live in various parts of the Near and Middle East, from Egypt, Greece, and Turkey to Syria, Iraq, Iran, and Armenia. They were also strongly associated with India and southern parts of the former Soviet Union.

Jawzahr

In ancient Persia, eclipses were said to occur when Jawzahr the comet dragon swallowed the sun or moon. He menaced the two great luminaries, chasing them around the sky and devouring them at regular intervals.

HEAD
Jawzahr's huge, horned head is able to live independently from his body. His eyes glint with perpetual malice.

JAWS
Gaping jaws capable of devouring the sun or moon in one gulp produce a furious screech that can be heard across a continent.

WINGS

Essential to carry him on his pursuit of the sun and moon, Jawzahr's wings contain a structure of lightweight but durable bone. A membrane of leathery skin is stretched across the framework of bone, giving Jawzahr the best aerodynamics of any known dragon.

TAIL

A spade-shaped tuft at the end of his tail indicates Jawzahr is a male. Female dragons lack this tuft.

CLAWS

Used for grasping tree branches or stone outcroppings back when he lived on Earth, Jawzahr's claws now grip at the air in a blind rage as he flies through the night skies.

Jawzahr is said to command a legion of demons. He is a crafty, curious dragon. According to legend, he disguised himself as a god one day and drank an immortality-giving potion meant only for the gods. The sun and moon, however, saw everything and reported Jawzahr's trickery to the gods. As punishment, Jawzahr's head was severed with one well-aimed throw of a discus. But Jawzahr was already immortal because of the potion he drank and could not be killed.

Enraged, Jawzahr ascended to the sky. He was angry at both the sun and the moon for revealing his deception to the gods.

Jawzahr is said to be forever chasing the sun and moon, gobbling them down when he catches them. Any time an eclipse occurs, it means that Jawzahr has caught up with and consumed the sun or the moon. As for his tail, it emits a shower of comets that stream across the night sky.

Did you know?

- The astronomical location of the dragon's head and dragon's tail mark the points where solar and lunar eclipses may occur.

- Draco, a constellation in the northern hemisphere, gets its name from the Latin word for dragon. One of the brightest stars in Draco is in its tail and is named Thuban, which is the Arabic word for dragon. Another star in Draco is Rastaban, which means "head of the dragon." About 5,000 years ago Thuban was the Pole Star, Earth's North Star. The ancient Egyptians recognized Thuban as the North Star at the time they were constructing the Great Pyramid. Today our North Star is Polaris.

- Many ancient cultures believed that comets were dragons streaking across the sky.

ACTUAL SIZE

Where in the World?

A dragon from Islamic mythology, Jawzahr first made his appearance in legends from Persia, which is modern-day Iran.

● IRAN

KRAKEN

Since medieval times, sailors and fishermen from western Europe—especially Scandinavia—have told of a vast, tentacled sea monster that lives in the ocean depths.

EYES
These provide superb vision, like the eyes of octopuses and squid.

HEADS
In many folk tales, the kraken is said to have three huge, identical heads.

TENTACLES
When a kraken surfaces, its long tentacles spread far across the water in all directions.

BEAK
Each head has a gaping chasm of a mouth, shaped like the beak of a parrot.

SUCKERS
Huge suckers on the rubbery tentacles hold a ship in a vise-like grip.

The kraken is a mountain of a creature, dwarfing the largest of whales. In a book on the natural history of Norway, published in 1754, the Bishop of Bergen claimed that the monster's body was almost 1½ miles in circumference.

The kraken is a sailor's worst nightmare. In the seas off northern Europe, a travel-weary captain might think he has sighted land at last. His charts make no reference to the strangely rounded islands, but he trusts his eyes and steers his ship toward them. But as he draws closer, the captain realizes his mistake with horror. The "islands" erupt from the sea to reveal a huge kraken.

The monster seizes the ship in a mighty tentacle and plunges it beneath the boiling waves. Grasping one of the crew with another tentacle, it lifts him, screaming, into a gaping beak.

Did you know?

- In some tales, the kraken has 1,000 tentacles and 10 mouths.

- There are reports of accidental kraken strandings. In 1680, a young kraken supposedly died after it was caught on the reefs off Alstadhang in Norway. In 1775, another was found on the Isle of Bute in Scotland.

- In the 1800's, the English poet Alfred Lord Tennyson wrote a poem, "The Kraken," inspired by the legends.

ACTUAL SIZE

Where in the World?

Most legends tell us the kraken lived around the coasts of Scandinavia, especially in the deep waters off Norway. But similar tales also come from other coastal areas of Europe.

● NORWAY

MINOTAUR

In Greek mythology, the Minotaur is born after King Minos angers the sea god Poseidon. Poseidon sends a snow-white bull for Minos to sacrifice, but Minos can't bring himself to kill the bull.

HEAD
The great, furry head and neck are those of a fearsome bull.

HORNS
Victims are gored to death by the beast's huge, curved horns.

EYES
Cold eyes glow with hatred.

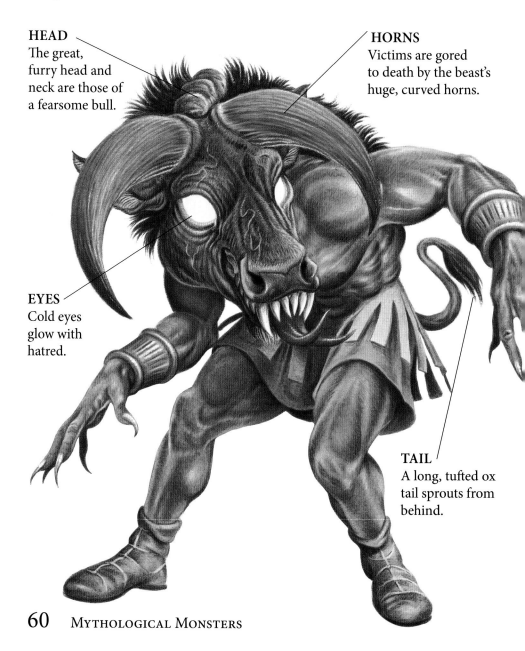

TAIL
A long, tufted ox tail sprouts from behind.

Poseidon punishes Minos by making his wife, Queen Pasiphae, fall in love with the bull. Pasiphae produces a child with a bull's head and a taste for human flesh. Minos orders the craftsman Daedalus to make a vast underground maze to house the monster.

In the story, the hero Theseus and his companions are sent from Athens as a sacrifice. Theseus, armed with a sword and a ball of thread, tells his men to stay near the maze's entrance while he searches for the Minotaur. After tying the end of the thread to a doorpost, Theseus picks his way through the maze, unraveling the ball as he goes. Suddenly, the beast is upon him! Summoning all his strength, Theseus plunges his sword through the Minotaur's neck, severing its head from its body. He then follows the thread back to the entrance of the maze.

ACTUAL SIZE

DID YOU KNOW?

- The story of Theseus slaying the Minotaur could be a symbolic version of real historical events, representing the Greek overthrow of Minoan power in 1450 B.C.

- Artifacts from ancient Crete show athletes performing the death-defying bull-leaping ceremony. Each athlete would face a wild, charging bull, grasp its spiked horns, and vault or somersault over the animal's back.

WHERE IN THE WORLD?

The mythical Minotaur was said to have lived at Knossos, on the island of Crete in the eastern Mediterranean. Theseus, who slew the beast, came from the city of Athens on the Greek mainland.

Ryujin

In Japanese mythology, Ryujin is the dragon god of the sea. He lives beneath the ocean in a jeweled palace made of red and white coral.

HEAD
His noble head bears the horns of a stag, whiskers that indicate his wisdom, and eyes that see everything from the very bottom of the ocean.

BODY
Ryujin winds his massive, scaly body through the chambers of his underwater palace far beyond the reach of any fisherman or scientist.

CLAWS
Floods result when Ryujin rakes his impressive claws through the ocean. A swipe of his foot is capable of capsizing an entire fleet of ships.

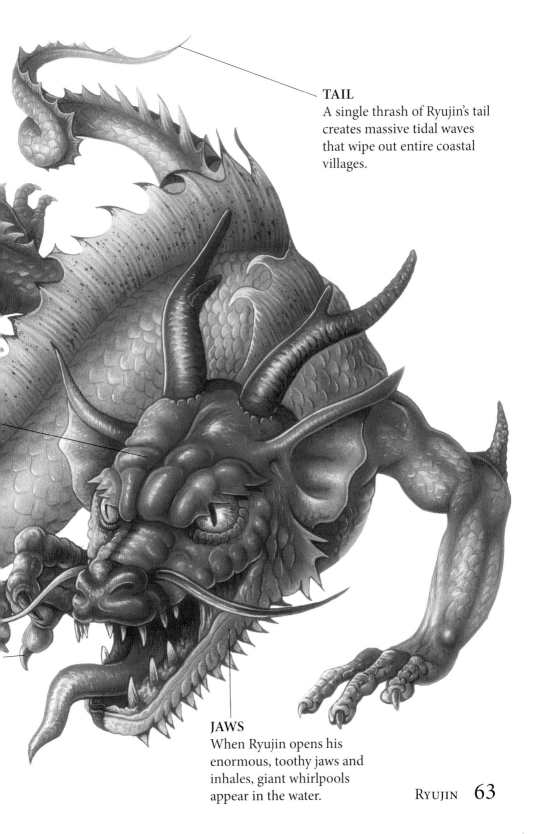

TAIL
A single thrash of Ryujin's tail creates massive tidal waves that wipe out entire coastal villages.

JAWS
When Ryujin opens his enormous, toothy jaws and inhales, giant whirlpools appear in the water.

Ryujin's palace is described as having a snowy winter hall, a spring hall where cherry trees grow, a summer hall with chirping crickets, and an autumn hall with colorful maple trees. For a human, one day at Ryujin's underwater palace is said to equal a hundred years on Earth. Sea turtles, fish, and jellyfish act as the dragon god's loyal servants. Ryujin controls the tides with magical sea jewels. Humans must approach Ryujin carefully because no mortal can glimpse his entire body and survive the sight. When he is angered, Ryujin churns the waves, causing rough waters for sailors. In one legend, the Empress Jingo plans to attack Korea and asks Ryujin for assistance. Ryujin's messenger brings her the two jewels that control the tides. Jingo sails toward Korea with the Japanese fleet. The Korean fleet meets them at sea. Jingo flings the low-tide jewel into the sea and all the waters disappear, stranding the Korean ships. When the Korean soldiers leap from their ships to attack on foot, Jingo casts the high-tide jewel onto the seabed. All the waters rush back, drowning the Korean soldiers.

DID YOU KNOW?

- Ryujin's beautiful daughter married Prince Hoori. This makes Ryujin the ancestor of all the Japanese emperors.

- Because Japanese dragons are related to royalty, no one is allowed to harm them. Because they have nothing to fear from humans, Japanese dragons have become tame over the years. Dragons may be seen blocking traffic in cities or sunning themselves on rocks off Japan's shores.

- Many dragons are shape-shifters. They can change into the form of a human, then mate and produce human offspring.

- In both Japan and China, the dragon is one of the guardian animals of the four directions. The dragon guards the eastern compass point and is associated with the season of spring.

ACTUAL SIZE

WHERE IN THE WORLD?

Ryujin, the dragon god of the sea, lives at the bottom of the ocean near the Ryukyu Islands off the coast of Japan.

JAPAN

Shen-Lung

In China, Shen-Lung is the spiritual dragon who is responsible for making weather.

BODY
Shen-Lung is a shape-shifter who can change his body into human form, stretch from heaven to Earth, or reduce himself to the size of a mouse.

JAWS
Shen-Lung exhales a breath of clouds that can become fire or rain. He basks in the sun with his whiskered jaws hanging open, hoping that a delicious sparrow will land in his mouth.

HEAD

Chinese dragons have the head of a camel, the eyes of a rabbit, the horns of a stag, and the ears of a bull.

CLAWS

Tiger paws bear the claws of an eagle. When Shen-Lung rakes his claws across another dragon during a midair fight, storms result.

Shen-Lung controls rain, clouds, and wind, all of which are important in a country with so many farmers. The right amount of rain is essential for healthy crops, so his power over rain gives Shen-Lung the authority over life and death in China. Offerings to Shen-Lung assure a bountiful harvest. He must be approached with respect and reverence. It is important not to offend Shen-Lung. The result of his wrath is terrible weather in the form of floods or drought, which could destroy the crops upon which the Chinese depend.

According to legend, Shen-Lung grew lazy over the years because of his great power. He is said to shrink himself to the size of a mouse in order to hide and avoid work. When lightning strikes a house or tree, it is the thunder god sending his servant to search for Shen-Lung. Shen-Lung floats across the sky, his body stretching farther than the eye can see. He is benevolent but bad-tempered.

DID YOU KNOW?

- Shen-Lung's voice is heard in hurricanes and his claws can be seen in flashes of lightning.

- When Shen-Lung is sick, the rain has a distinctly fishy smell.

- The dragon is the emblem representing the Chinese emperor and the phoenix represents the empress. Together, the dragon and the phoenix are used as symbols of marital harmony.

- All Chinese dragons have nine distinct features: the head of a camel, the scales of a carp, the horns of a stag, the eyes of a rabbit, the ears of a bull, the neck of a snake, the belly of a clam, the paws of a tiger, and the claws of an eagle.

- The dragon ranks first in the Chinese mythological hierarchy of 360 scaled creatures.

ACTUAL SIZE

WHERE IN THE WORLD?

Shen-Lung is the spiritual dragon who has control over the winds and the rains that affect all the crops grown in China.

● CHINA

SPHINX

This cruel monster of legend challenges all who try to pass her to solve a riddle—then slaughters and devours them when they get the answer wrong!

WINGS
Huge wings carry the beast up to her mountaintop, from where she can survey the land and swoop down on people.

TAIL
In many versions of the story, the Sphinx has a snake for a tail. One bite from its venomous fangs is enough to bring down even the strongest and most determined challenger.

HIND LEGS
These are powerfully muscled for leaping at victims the moment they answer her riddle incorrectly, giving them no chance whatsoever of fleeing to safety.

BODY
Some accounts say the Sphinx had the body of an enormous dog, but most describe it as being the body of a lioness in her prime. It ripples with muscle built up from vast and regular meals of fresh human flesh.

HEAD
The Sphinx has the head of a woman, with foul fangs to tear her victims limb from limb.

CLAWS
Wickedly long and sharp, these pin victims to the ground and rip open their skin.

FOREPAWS
The Sphinx holds victims down with her huge clawed paws, and then crushes their windpipes with single massive bites.

Myths describe the Sphinx as a horrible creature with the head of a woman, an eagle's wings, the body of a lioness, and a snake for a tail. She terrorizes the poor people of Thebes in Greece from her domain on a mountaintop. No one can pass the Sphinx unless they correctly answer her riddle. Should a challenger answer incorrectly, the Sphinx will pounce on him, pin him to the ground, and clamp her teeth around his throat.

She is finally killed by the Greek hero Oedipus, who marches straight up to the monster in her lair on Mount Phicium and demands to hear her riddle. Fixing him with her steely gaze, she chants in a sing-song voice: "What walks with four legs in the morning, two at noon, and three in the evening?" To her complete amazement, Oedipus answers confidently and correctly: "A man." Enraged, the Sphinx hurls herself off the mountain and falls screaming to her death in the valley below.

Did you know?

- "Sphinx" means "strangler" and comes from the ancient Greek verb "sphingo," meaning "to throttle."

- Since it was carved more than 4,000 years ago, the Great Sphinx in Egypt has spent most of its time buried up to its neck in sand. The head has been badly worn by weathering and at some point it lost its beard and nose. Also, the troops of French Emperor Napoleon Bonaparte (1769–1821) used the monument for target practice.

ACTUAL SIZE

Where in the World?

Depictions of Sphinxes are known from all over the eastern Mediterranean. In the Greek legend, the Sphinx came from Ethiopia and lived on Mount Phicium, which may be Mount Parnassus, in Thebes in Greece.

THEBES

THUNDERBIRD

This gigantic two-headed bird of prey is known by many American Indian tribes to bring thunder and lightning to the skies.

EYES
Each time the thunderbird opens its eyes, bolts of lightning flash in the sky.

BACK
The thunderbird can carry an entire lake on its mighty back, releasing the water in torrential downpours.

HEADS
A second head sprouts from the thunderbird's chest. Both heads are equipped with viciously hooked beaks.

Stories tell us that lightning bolts shoot from the thunderbird's eyes, storm clouds are carried on its wings, and a lake on its back makes torrential downpours. Yet the thunderbird means different things to different American Indian tribes. Some tribes believe that the thunderbird is the Great Creator Spirit that made the heavens and the earth.

The Nootka people of Vancouver Island, off British Columbia, called the thunderbird Tootooch. To them, it was the sole survivor of four giant birds that preyed on whales. In the tales of the Quillayute people of the Olympic Peninsula in Washington State, the thunderbird and killer whale are deadly enemies.

ACTUAL SIZE

WINGS
Powerful wings with feathers as long as canoe paddles send claps of thunder echoing through the air.

FEET
Huge, curved talons tip each toe, like those of a giant eagle or vulture.

DID YOU KNOW?

- Members of many American Indian tribes claim to have seen the thunderbird, and in South Dakota they believe it left huge footprints. The prints are 25 miles apart in an area known as Thunder Tracks, near the source of St. Peter's River.

- Some stories say that the thunderbird lives in a mountain cave.

WHERE IN THE WORLD?

Thunderbirds are part of the belief systems that were held by many different American Indian groups, from the Inuit peoples in the Arctic to the Aztecs in Mexico. These gigantic birds are thought to live either in the sky or in remote mountain caves.

BIGFOOT

This terrifying, apelike creature is said to roam remote mountain forests, but it has eluded researchers for more than 150 years. Standing well over 6 ½ feet high, with arms down to its knees, Bigfoot can easily carry away dogs and livestock. More than 1,600 reports of Bigfoot sightings have been recorded in the United States and Canada since the early 1800's.

FACE
Bigfoot has a heavy brow ridge and wide, apelike nostrils. Its eyes may shine green or yellow.

SIZE
Bigfoot measures more than 3 ¼ feet wide, and has a stooping posture and broad, sloping shoulders. It is estimated to weigh between 400 and 440 pounds.

ARMS
The arms are long in proportion to the body, hanging down to the knees or even below.

HAIR
One of Bigfoot's most distinctive features is a thick covering of hair. Usually, this coat is shaggy and brown, but some people have described rust-colored, black, or even glossy hair.

GIGANTOPITHECUS

YETI

Creatures similar to Bigfoot are reported in other parts of the world:

Gigantopithecus: This giant ape was the largest primate ever to live on Earth. Fossils of two species have been found in India and China, dating from between one and nine million years ago. Scientists think the ape lived in open country, but they don't know if it walked upright.

Yeti: Although there have been few actual sightings of the Himalayan abominable snowman, or Yeti, many people have come across its distinctive tracks. Some who have seen the Yeti describe a creature with pale or white hair, but others report a darker coat and a pointed head.

Alma: This "wild man" of Central Asia is reputedly smaller than Bigfoot and less apelike in build. In the late 1950's, Soviet scientist Boris Porshnev suggested that these "wild men" were remnant populations of Neandertals.

ALMA

DID YOU KNOW?

- Many people who have shot at Bigfoot from point-blank range report that the creature seems invulnerable to gunfire.

- In 1995, a sample of alleged Bigfoot hair was sent for DNA analysis to the Ohio State University. After years of testing, the results are still inconclusive.

- Hunters claim their dogs whimper and shy away from Bigfoot.

ACTUAL SIZE

WHERE IN THE WORLD?

More than 400 reports of Bigfoot sightings come from the American states of California, Oregon, and Washington, and from British Columbia, Canada. Sightings have been reported in almost every part of Canada and the United States.

CHUPACABRA

A modern menace of the Americas, farmers and authorities alike blame this bloodsucking, batlike fiend for the brutal slaughter of pets and livestock.

EYES
The size of a hen's eggs, the monster's big eyes glow an alien red. Some witnesses claim they fire laser beams to paralyze victims!

CLAWS
The monster's feet and hands have huge, viciously curved and wickedly sharp claws for pinning down helpless prey.

LEGS
These are long and muscular for bounding 66 feet at a stride when advancing on prey. Strangely, the monster never leaves footprints.

SPINES

These reportedly burst through the skin of the monster's head and back. Their purpose is unknown, but they may offer protection against enemies.

SIZE

Eyewitness accounts are muddled. Estimates of the creature's height vary from 3 feet to 6 ½ feet.

WINGS

The chupacabra is usually said to have batlike wings with a span of up to 13 feet. A few reports say it has no wings.

SKIN

Some witnesses say the beast has bare gray or blue skin, others that it has scales or fur.

FANGS

Witnesses say the chupacabra's mouth bristles with great fangs. Some say they are bright red.

Stories tell how a chupacabra attack might occur: The beast swoops toward a herd of goats and drops silently between the trees. Sensing danger, the goats bleat in panic as the monster approaches. Paralyzed by terror and the foul, sulfurous odor of the chupacabra, the goats are helpless. The monster seizes the nearest one with its claws, plunges its huge fangs into the animal, and swiftly sucks out every last drop of blood. Goat after goat, it drains the herd, then slips off in search of other prey.

This fanged, spined, foul-smelling monster was first reported in 1995. It is believed to seek out its victims in the dark of night and prey on a range of farm and domestic animals, sucking them dry of blood. Its name means "goat-sucker," after its first victim. Some people say that the chupacabra comes from outer space, while others say it is the result of U.S. military experiments.

Did you know?

- Two Brazilian fishermen claim they shot a chupacabra dead and still have its head—which they refuse to let anyone examine.

- The mayor of Canóvanas, a town in Puerto Rico, leads chupacabra search parties, armed with a crucifix and a gun. He also sets traps around the town in the hope of catching one of the elusive creatures.

- In 1996, a Mexican policeman opened fire on a chupacabra at close range. However, his bullets had no effect and the monster escaped.

- Attacks on humans are rare, but a nurse in Mexico reportedly lost an arm to the fangs of a chupacabra.

ACTUAL SIZE

Where in the World?

The chupacabra is known in Central and South America. There are also reports from California, Arizona, Texas, and Florida in the United States. Most sightings are from Puerto Rico, an island about 1,000 miles southeast of Florida.

PUERTO RICO

GLAURUNG

Glaurung the Deceiver casts spells
that create misery and confusion.

TAIL
Glaurung's whiplike tail is a
deadly weapon. A blow dealt
by Glaurung's tail can crumble
stone walls or snap a grown
man's spine.

BODY
A glimmer of fire shows
around the edges
of his golden,
armorlike scales when
Glaurung is enraged.
His scales fade to a dull
gray when his fury dies
down. Only the dragon's
slimy belly, which lacks
scales, is vulnerable to
attack.

JAWS
Flames as hot as lava shoot from Glaurung's
jaws, scorching everything nearby. When not
spouting fire, his breath has the distinctly putrid
reek of decaying animal flesh.

The English writer J.R.R. Tolkien describes how Glaurung, who was bred by Morgoth the Enemy, uses trickery and deception. The dragon wreaks as much havoc casting spells as he does using brute force on the battlefield. He serves as the eyes of Morgoth, who senses everything the dragon sees.

Glaurung casts spells with his lidless, unblinking eyes. He bewitches the heroic Túrin with lies and self-doubt. Túrin's sister, Nienor, is also victim of Glaurung's spell—she is unable to remember who she is and unwittingly marries her brother. Túrin clings to a cliffside above a gorge where Glaurung passes. When the dragon slithers overhead, Túrin kills Glaurung by thrusting his sword into the beast's soft belly.

ACTUAL SIZE

EYES
Lidless, unblinking eyes cast a spell that renders his victims helpless. Everything Glaurung sees is telepathically transmitted to his master, Morgoth.

DID YOU KNOW?

- Glaurung generates a horrible reek and foul vapors that blind people until they lose their way. Even horses are driven mad by the dragon's stench.

- Anyone foolish enough to look Glaurung directly in the eye is immediately rendered helpless by his dragon spell.

WHERE IN THE WORLD?

Glaurung is the first and fiercest of the land-dwelling firedrakes of Middle Earth described in J.R.R. Tolkien's *The Silmarillion*. Glaurung builds a nest upon the treasure in the tunnels beneath Nargothrond after the city is sacked.

NARGOTHROND

Middle Earth

JERSEY DEVIL

The bleak marshes of New Jersey in the United States have never welcomed people, and locals tell of strange sightings and chilling cries in the dark. According to many people, something evil is out there. With batlike wings and the head of a deformed horse, this inexplicable beast has been terrifying locals for more than 200 years.

WINGS
The leathery wings resemble those of a bat, and some say their span is surprisingly small, stretching to just 26 inches when fully unfurled.

BODY
The body is that of a dog or horse. Its lithe, muscular form emits a yellowish hue as the beast flies at night.

TAIL
Some say its tail is tipped with a tuft; others say it ends with a three-pointed spike.

HIND LEGS
The Jersey Devil often walks upright on its two hind legs, which some witnesses describe as being long and spindly like those of a crane.

HEAD

The creature's head is similar to that of a donkey, but with a dog's nose and teeth. Its gums are rotten and its breath is so foul that it curdles milk, blights crops, and poisons rivers and lakes, killing fish.

HORNS

Two goatlike horns top the creature's head, enhancing its devilish appearance.

FORELEGS

Each leg ends in a cloven hoof, but the forelegs are relatively short and stubby and are seldom used.

Stories tell how the Jersey Devil, driven mad by hunger, leaves its dismal swampy home and flies to nearby towns. After cruising over the rooftops, it spots a suitable chimney and dives swiftly down the soot-laden stack. The devil is unscathed by the fierce fire burning in the grate and bursts through the flames, scattering logs into the kitchen beyond. As the devil makes for the larder, anyone nearby can only pray that the food there will satisfy the beast. Witnesses of the devil's approach are advised to remain silent—a single cry might tempt the ravenous beast to sample fresher food.

The devil is said to emerge in the dead of night to haunt the countryside, killing wild and domestic animals and abducting small children. In January 1909, more than 1,000 people said they came face-to-face with the Jersey Devil in a single week. The beast appeared to householders, policemen, and local officials. The accounts were all very similar, and local and national newspapers were forced to take the story seriously.

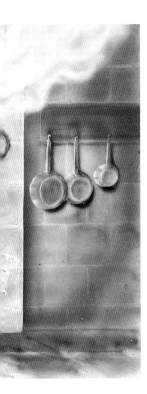

Did you know?

■ In 1909, the Philadelphia Zoo offered a $10,000 reward for the capture of the devil. This prompted several hoaxes, including a painted kangaroo with a set of false wings. The reward has yet to be claimed.

■ When the rotting corpse of a strange, devilish creature was found in the Pine Barrens in 1957, many people took this as evidence that the Jersey Devil was dead. However, there have been several sightings since then.

ACTUAL SIZE

Where in the World?

Many sightings of the Jersey Devil occur in the Pine Barrens of New Jersey—a lonely area of swamps and cedar forests covering 1,698 square miles. Other reports come from all around the state, and occasionally from across the border.

NEW JERSEY ●

LOCH NESS

Legend has long had it that something strange lurks in the dark depths of Loch Ness, a lake in northern Scotland. Since the 1930's, thousands of people have claimed to have seen a hump-backed, long-necked beast there.

NECK
Like some plesiosaurs, Nessie is said to have a long, flexible neck—ideal for twisting and turning after fleeing fish.

FLIPPERS
A pair of flippers front and back propel the beast through the water like a penguin or turtle.

TAIL
A stubby tail was a typical feature of plesiosaurs.

HEAD
Forward-pointing eyes allow the monster to target fish. Nessie also needs plenty of needle-sharp teeth to seize slippery, wriggling prey.

Some people claim that the "Loch Ness Monster" (sometimes called "Nessie") is a plesiosaur, a prehistoric ocean reptile that went extinct about 65 million years ago. They say it lived at sea until after the last Ice Age, then adapted to the fresh water of Loch Ness. Other people think Nessie could be a type of fish called a sturgeon. These enormous fish sometimes swim up the River Ness from the sea and enter the loch in search of food or mates. These fish can be several feet in length, with lines of prominent humps on their backs. Other people believe the monster is nothing more than a large eel.

Whatever the reality, the fact remains that numerous people have claimed to have seen the monster. Even today the loch attracts tourists hoping to catch sight of Nessie.

ACTUAL SIZE

Did you know?

- There is not a single recorded sighting of Nessie before 1930.

- Several people have reported seeing Nessie on land. On July 22, 1933, a husband and wife reported that a monster crossed the road in front of their car as they drove along the loch.

- Scientists who believe the Loch Ness Monster exists have given it a Latin name: *Nessitera rhombopteryx*.

Where in the World?

Loch Ness is part of a chain of lochs, rivers, and canals in the Great Glen, a geological fault that runs across the Scottish Highlands from the North Sea to the Atlantic Ocean. The River Ness links the loch to the North Sea.

● LOCH NESS

SMAUG

Isolated deep within the Lonely Mountain, Smaug the Golden sleeps atop the pile of treasure that he stole from the dwarves.

JAWS
Smaug's fiery breath at full force reduces every building in town to a heap of ashes. He produces a roar that is so fierce and deafening it causes avalanches.

BODY
Nothing, not a sword nor arrow nor curse, can penetrate Smaug's tough hide. However, there is one spot on his underside that is vulnerable.

EYES
Blazing eyes emit a thin, piercing red beam that casts a dragon spell.

WINGS
A noise like a roaring wind is produced by the flapping of Smaug's enormous wings.

TAIL
A single sweep of Smaug's mighty tail is all it takes to smash the roof of Esgaroth's Great House.

LEGS
Muscular legs trample the ground with enough force to shake the roots of mountains. His claws are capable of crushing boulders.

In *The Hobbit,* the English writer J.R.R. Tolkien describes Smaug's lair, which lies at the end of a mountain tunnel in a dungeon hall dug by dwarves. His lair gives off an eerie red glow and emits wisps of vapor. Smaug makes his bed on the mass of treasure that he hoards. He lies upon the gems for so long that they stick to his soft belly, forming a dazzling protective armor.

Near the end of the novel, Bilbo the hobbit is able to sneak in and steal a cup from the treasure hoard. The theft infuriates Smaug. He circles the sky above the mountain in a rage, bellowing and shooting flames. Later, Bilbo makes himself invisible and sneaks into the dragon's cave again. Although Smaug cannot see Bilbo, he can smell him and he mocks the invisible hobbit. Bilbo flatters the vain Smaug into rolling over onto his back. Bilbo spots an open patch in Smaug's jeweled armor. Knowledge of his weak spot is passed on to Bard the Bowman, who kills Smaug with a single arrow.

DID YOU KNOW?

- It is unwise to reveal one's true name to a dragon.

- Many experts believe that a dragon is able to breathe fire because it stores a mixture of gases in its body. These gases ignite upon contact with the air, producing an intense flame.

- The dragon's ability to store such gases as methane may account for its terrible stench.

- There is no record of any dragon dying of old age. All dragons in recorded history have died from accidents, disease, or battle injuries.

- Dragons have heightened senses of smell, sight, and hearing. Some breeds can see objects as far as a mile away and hear sounds well outside the range of the human ear.

ACTUAL SIZE

WHERE IN THE WORLD?

Smaug is the last of the great dragons of Middle Earth in J.R.R. Tolkien's *The Hobbit*. His lair is deep within Lonely Mountain.

● LONELY MOUNTAIN

Index